Based on the true tale of her own talented pet's experience coping with the new baby in the house, Newbery Award—winning author Madeleine L'Engle now treats the youngest readers to a familiar domestic drama with an utterly charming new twist. And Christine Davenier's lively pictures tell Touché's story with all the flair and wit of this most precocious poodle.

"Any family with a cosseted dog and a new baby will feel this is written just for them."
—*Publishers Weekly*

"Young listeners . . . will find this very funny; adults . . . will be touched."
—*Booklist*

Madeleine L'Engle

The O[T]

HER DOG

Illustrated by

Christine Davenier

chronicle books · san francisco

Typeset in Fontesque and Locarno.
Manufactured in Hong Kong.

Library of Congress Cataloging-in-Publication Data
L'Engle, Madeleine.
The other dog / Madeleine L'Engle ; illustrated by Christine Davenier.— 1st paperback ed.
p. cm.
Summary: The family poodle protests at first when the master and mistress bring home a new "dog" to share the household.
ISBN-13: 978-0-8118-5228-9 (13-digit)
ISBN-10: 0-8118-5228-8 (10-digit)
[1. Dogs—Fiction. 2. Babies—Fiction.] I. Davenier, Christine, ill. II. Title.
PZ7.L5385Ot 2006
[E]—dc22
2005018705

Distributed in Canada by Raincoast Books
9050 Shaughnessy Street, Vancouver, British Columbia V6P 6E5

10 9 8 7 6 5 4 3 2 1

Chronicle Books LLC
85 Second Street, San Francisco, California 94105

www.chroniclekids.com

For my great-grandsons,
Konstantinos John Voiklis and Cooper Hindemith Roy,
who bring light to all the dark corners
—Madeleine L'Engle

For my daughter, Josephine
—Christine Davenier

First of all,

I think you should know that
I am the one who **wrote** this book.
After all (contrary to opinion),
the author of a book is very **important**.
Please believe me: without the author,
a book would **never get written.**
So, I—Touché L'Engle-Franklin—

wrote this book,

with the assistance of that

inferior canine

Jo.

This summer . . .

my mistress went away for **several days.**
And when she came back, she brought with her

another dog.

If you ask me, this was a great waste of money.
Dogs are expensive to feed and clothe,
and one dog is enough for any family.
I fail to see why I did not satisfy **all** requirements.

I have beauty, wit, and charm.

I have been on the stage.

I am very talented.

And until this other dog
was brought into our home
(without warning),
my master and mistress
seemed perfectly happy with me.

I am **very good** about sitting on **laps**.
In fact, I **love** sitting on laps.
I know of no other dog
who could sit on a lap for as **long** as
or with as much **patience** as I can.

So why another dog?

I dance, oh-so-daintily,

when it is time to eat.

My master and mistress
love to look at me.

So why another dog?

I afford my master endless pleasure in his off-hours
when he bathes and clips me.
I can wear my ears long or short.
I sit still for hours while he snips off hair here and there.
No other dog would be so good and patient.

I am tremendously **useful** in such household tasks
as bringing home the groceries.
And I **always** tell my master and mistress
when the telephone or the doorbell rings.
No one could be
more efficient,
more energetic,
more conscientious,
or **louder**
about this than I am.

So why another dog?

But what's done is done.
The dog was brought home, and I had to learn
to make the best of it.

Nevertheless, from the start I noticed
a great many mysterious and horrifying things.
For instance,
when I am taken out to get some fresh air
I always have to walk—even when it rains.
The Jo is taken out in a carriage,
and when it rains
she doesn't have to go out at all.

And **another** thing.

My master and mistress keep putting on

and taking off white pieces of cloth around Jo's bottom,

called, for some obscure reason, diapers.

At first I did not understand the significance of this.

But when I did, I was deeply shocked.

When I have anything of that sort to do,

I go out into the street.

White cloths or no, I would **never** do it in the house.

At least one thing remained clear.

Of the two dogs, I was the most important.

You see, each night we would start out in our separate beds,

this dog called Jo, and I.

(Now, her bed may be a little more fancy and froufrou,

but mine is more practical.)

In the morning she would still be in her bed,
but I would not be in my bed.
Well, if that doesn't show you who's who around here,
I don't know what would.

And another thing.
This Jo-dog gets fed **several** times a day.
I only get fed **once**.
Of course, there may be a **reason** for this.

You see, I have frequently been told
that my tail is like a little chrysanthemum.
Jo-thing hasn't any tail at all.
Of course I am aware that, because of the dictates of fashion,
some dogs have their tails clipped.
But there is always something left.
And Jo has no tail.
Perhaps they think that if they feed her
and feed her,
she may grow a beautiful chrysanthemummy tail like mine.

And, by the way, our Jo—as well as having no tail—
has practically no hair.
Certainly not enough to brush.
So, when people come to call,
we have to put clothes on her.
All I need is a good hairbrushing.

If summer comes, can fall be far behind?
So said the poet.
Came autumn, and Jo-girl and I are almost the same size.
She has a little more hair but not much.
I am afraid she is just of an inferior breed called "baby,"
and there is nothing that can be done about it.

When the Jo-dog grew bigger
and bigger every day, and more and more **rambunctious,**
my master and mistress got a doghouse for her—
something I have been well-behaved enough **never** to need.
And now, when company comes,
I have to stay at the doghouse
and watch over our Jo.

I guess I have become more use there
than as the life of the party.
Ho hum . . .
It may be useful, but it's not nearly as much **fun.**
But since we have Jo-dog,
someone has to take care of her,
and I will do my part.

I must admit, though, that in our few conversations
she's been most interested in everything I've had to say—

which is, I think, a definitely encouraging sign of
intelligence.

Therefore, I must admit that
in spite of myself . . .
in spite of the Jo-girl . . .
in spite of everything . . .
I am getting very fond of our other dog.
So, somehow or other, I have come to the
unpredictable,
surprising,
amazing,
astonishing,
astounding conclusion:

in every home there should be

at least

two dogs!

So now good-bye——and lots of love.
Touché

Touché, a little grey poodle, came into my life when she was bought—for an exorbitant sum, I thought—during the rehearsals for Eva Le Gallienne's production of Chekhov's *The Cherry Orchard*. Of course, all the actors with dogs had wanted their pets in the show, but these other dogs were either intimidated by being in the theatre or, if they passed that first test, were undone by the noise of the party scene. So in came Touché, a born actress who wasn't in the least intimidated by the laughter and song of the party scene; she was quickly hired. Someone had to take care of her before and after the show, and I (the general understudy, who did everything that wasn't specified in the script) was lucky enough to get the job.

By the time the show was over, Touché and I had definitely "bonded," and there was no taking her away from me. By that time, Touché was thoroughly addicted to the adulation she received on stage. "Oh, that marvelous little dog! How did you teach her? She trains so easily! Can't you give her a little more to do? The audience adores her in that scene when she jumps up and tries to comfort—"

At this point Eva Le Gallienne would protest, a little wistfully, "That's supposed to be my scene." I could understand Le Gallienne's point of view.

There were a few less easily solved problems. For instance, travel. I lived in Greenwich Village. The theatre was in midtown. There was no way I could afford, on my Equity minimum salary, to take Touché back and forth in a taxi. So what to do?

I thought it over, and then I slung her over my shoulders like a feather boa, and she obediently hung there until we got to the stage door alley. Wherever I went, Touché went with me.

When Hugh Franklin was cast as Petya Trofimov, the young student who is Chekhov's mouthpiece, I expected the usual jealous annoyance from Touché. Not at all. Touché gave Hugh an appraising look, an interested sniff, and decided that he was all right. To my surprise, she let him brush her. She chose him to be her groom.

She did not come to our tiny little wedding, but otherwise she was with us night and day. And every evening, at the close of the play, she had her own special curtain call. We had to cut her down to one curtain call only, because she danced around and waved her paws at the audience and tended to take over the show, and the other actors complained.

When we had our first baby, I sat on the sofa nursing her, and Touché sat beside me, nursing a pink rubber hippopotamus. When she had her first litter, she was less concerned about the puppies than she was about her hippopotamus. She did her duty, but she wasn't really interested. But Touché and the puppies were so charming together that I took colored pencils and began sketching them. And that was the beginning of this book.

Her first love remained her true love: the theatre. There are not a great many roles written for a small grey poodle, but she did play Flush, Elizabeth Barrett's spaniel, in *The Barretts of Wimpole Street*. There's no way Touché looked like a spaniel; we just counted on her acting ability. The show had a long run, and Touché was happy. After it closed, everybody wanted to take Touché home—but she was mine, there was no questioning that.

There were no more plays at that time with dogs

in the cast. But she had the best of everything that I could give her—a warm green wool coat in cold weather, and little boots for mud. She hated the boots, so I stopped fighting her about them. *I* might not want to go barefooted in winter weather, but then, I don't have fur between my toes.

She ate well: we gave her ground beef, not the prepared ground beef, full of fat, but specially ground top round. If she was "off her feed," I fed her by hand. Unlike most dogs, her theatre training had taught her to like the spotlight—even for her private functions, she sought a street lamp before she squatted to pee. And we were expected to have tissues ready to wipe her for bigger business. And when she had accomplished everything, she expected applause.

She lived with us happily until her kidneys failed, and she died quietly one night, lying between us on our bed. An era was ended, and things would never be the same.

—MADELEINE L'ENGLE

Madeleine L'Engle is the author of more than forty books for children, including her Newbery Award—winning title, *A Wrinkle in Time*, and its companion pieces, *A Wind in the Door*, *A Swiftly Tilting Planet*, and *Many Waters*. She has also written numerous adult novels and several autobiographic and theological books.

After the success of her first novel, *The Small Rain*, Ms. L'Engle continued writing full-time, and with her husband and three children, she divided her time between their two homes in New York City and Connecticut. She is now the writer-in-residence and a volunteer librarian at the Cathedral of St. John the Divine in New York City.

Christine Davenier has illustrated a number of children's books, including *I Love the Rain* and *I Heard It from Alice Zuchini* (both available from Chronicle Books), *Mabel Dancing*, *Leon and Albertine*, *The Low-Down Laundry Line Blues*, and *Very Best (almost) Friends: Poems of Friendship*. She lives with her husband and daughter in Paris, France.